Amory Howe Bradford

The Sistine Madonna

A Christmas Meditation

Amory Howe Bradford

The Sistine Madonna
A Christmas Meditation

ISBN/EAN: 9783742862648

Manufactured in Europe, USA, Canada, Australia, Japa

Cover: Foto ©Andreas Hilbeck / pixelio.de

Manufactured and distributed by brebook publishing software
(www.brebook.com)

Amory Howe Bradford

The Sistine Madonna

The Sistine Madonna

A Christmas Meditation

BY

AMORY H. BRADFORD

NEW-YORK

FORDS, HOWARD, & HULBERT

1900

The Madonna and Child.

Written after viewing Raphael's Madonna di San Sisto
in the Royal Gallery of Dresden, August, 1867.

Thou stand'st between the earth and heaven,
  Sweet Mary, with thy boy;
And on thy young and lovely face
  Linger surprise and joy.

The angel's words are sounding yet
  In thy attentive ear;
Thou hold'st thy child most tenderly,
  And yet with awe and fear.

Almost a frightened look thou hast,
  As if within thy thought
The glory of thy motherhood
  An anxious burden brought.

Thou dar'st not clasp the Holy Child
  With freedom to thy breast;
And yet, because he is thine own,
  Thou look'st supremely blest.

God gave the boy into thine arms,
  And thou his mother art,
And yet the words the angel spoke
  Are lingering in thy heart.

GRACE WEBSTER HINSDALE.

The Madonna to her Child.

It is enough to bear
This image still and fair,
This holier in sleep
Than a saint at prayer;
This aspect of a child
Who never sinned or smiled;
This presence in an infant's face:
This sadness most like love,
This love than love more deep,
This weakness like omnipotence,
It is so strong to move!
Awful is this watching place,
Awful what I see from hence —
A king without regalia,
A God without the thunder,
A child without the heart for play:
Ay, a Creator rent asunder
From his first glory, and cast away
On his own world, for me alone
To hold in hands created, crying, Son!

ELIZABETH BARRETT BROWNING.

7

And when they were come into the house, they saw the young child with Mary his mother, and fell down, and worshipped him.

MATTHEW ii. 11.

The Sistine Madonna:

A CHRISTMAS MEDITATION.

DIFFERENT men have different gifts. One approaches truth through a process of reasoning; his expression of it is always in logical forms. We call that man a philosopher or a theologian. Another has a sensitive spirit; to him ideas have the vividness of present realities. We call him a seer. What one finds as the result of long and laborious steps, the other sees. The Hebrew prophets were seers. They expressed truth in picturesque and rhythmical forms.   Not one of them resembled a modern theologian.   The scribes were theologians; the prophets were men who saw truth intuitively and uttered it poetically.   Whittier was more like Isaiah than any man of our time, both as to thought and mode of expression.   Others see and express truth in concord of sweet sounds.   A certain great musician, when he wished to pray, would go into the dark and silent church, and seating himself at his organ, let its majestic tones voice his petition and his praise.   Some men have been inspired to preach, like Paul; some to sing, like David and Isaiah; and some have been inspired to utter truth neither in logical nor in rhythmical forms, but to paint.   A picture may be an expression of doctrine as truly as a logical treatise or a poem. Especially in the period succeeding the Middle Ages great souls found expression on canvas for the profoundest spiritual truths; hence the galleries of Europe are full of Madonnas, Nativities, Crucifixions, Ascensions.

There are two ways of thinking of the masterpieces of the world's art. One is to see in them simply pictures, representations of men, women, and children; the other is to view them as symbols—attempts to put into form what those who have vision see with the spirit's eye. Among the great master-artists the two greatest, Michelangelo and Raphael, according to the standards of their age, were men of lofty character; and their works show that much of their time must have been spent in the contemplation of the life and death of our Lord.

The most beautiful picture in the world is the Sistine Madonna in the Royal Gallery at Dresden, Saxony. It was painted by Raphael as an altar-piece for a church in Piacenza, Italy. In a far corner room in the great Palace of Art in Dresden it is now placed, probably to remain until the colors shall fade from the canvas. It is the only piece in the room. The figures are of life size. When that room is entered all voices are hushed, and all merriment silenced. The place is as holy as a church. In the center of the canvas is the Virgin Mother, with a young, almost girlish face of surpassing loveliness. In her eyes affection and wonder are blended, and the features and the figure are the most spiritual and beautiful in the world's art.

I have wondered where Raphael found that face. It is not voluptuous like the Italian, nor heavy like the German, nor light like the French, nor cold like the women of more northern nations. It is the ideal woman's face for all nations and ages, and yet it is typical of none.

In the Mother's arms is the Divine Child, with those strange, far-away-looking eyes that casual visitors so little understand — eyes that even in babyhood seem reading the future and beginning to see the greatness of the world's sorrow. Kneeling on one side below them is St. Sixtus, the nearest perfect of all pictures of strong and venerable age that were ever painted; on the other side Santa Barbara, only less beautiful than the Virgin, is kneeling, with eyes turned from the glory too bright for mortals to look upon. At the bottom of the canvas are the two cherub faces which for centuries have been ideals of innocence and loveliness. The background is of fleecy clouds, and peering out of the clouds are angel faces.

It has been said that Raphael never painted anything exactly as it was, but always idealized whatever he touched. If he found those faces anywhere among the throngs in Italian streets, he lifted them out of their surroundings and glorified them, so that all nations recognize in that matchless Madonna their ideal of the Mother of our Lord, and in that child their ideal of the Divine Child. The vision of angels breaking the barriers of physical limitations and entering human spheres is a suggestion that the spiritual and physical are never far apart, and that perhaps if we had clearer vision, angel faces might be often seen, and if we had more acute hearing, angel songs would be often heard. This greatest of all paintings conveys immortal lessons in a pictorial and impressive form.

The central figure at the Advent and in the childhood of Christ was his mother. In the painting, too, the mother is not less prominent than her child. The Roman Church has carried its adoration of the Virgin too far, but Protestants have treated her with positive neglect. Raphael has made her the most beautiful woman ever dreamed of by art. Perhaps he was right. Who knows? Of hardly any other prominent character in history is there so little recorded as of Mary. Luke alone of the Evangelists even mentions her place of residence. Probably she was one of those modest and sweetly beautiful souls that grow in seclusion like flowers among mountains. There is nothing finer in this world of ours than pure and modest maidenhood. Unto such an one came the mysterious message that she was to be a mother—by the direct power of God; and all we know of her at this time is that she was troubled at the announcement, and wondered what it could mean. The Jews believed in angelic ministries. It could have occasioned her no surprise that an angel should speak: the wonder was that the word should have come to her. But when the Annunciation came, with sweet submissiveness she replied: "Behold the handmaid of the Lord; be it unto me according to thy word."

The most retiring spirits sometimes speak the loftiest thoughts; so Mary, before the birth of her child, her mind saturated with the poetry of her people, breaks forth into one of the noblest songs of the ages, which in its

Latin translation has been for hundreds of years a peculiarly splendid part of the Catholic Church service under the name of the " Magnificat":

My soul doth magnify the Lord,
And my spirit hath rejoiced in God my Saviour.
For he hath regarded the low estate of his
    handmaiden : for, behold, from henceforth all
    generations shall call me blessed.

The next we read of Mary was at the Advent, when to the exquisite wonder of motherhood was added the awe caused by the coming of the shepherds and their adoration. And then we are given but a hint of the effect of these experiences: " But Mary kept all these things, and pondered them in her heart."

And so the story moves on, affording only here and there a glimpse of the mother of our Lord. At the Presentation in the Temple, when Simeon uttered that impassioned "Nunc Dimittis," we read, "they marvelled." And well they might! What strange thoughts must have filled that mother's heart, when the venerable prophet foretold great things for her boy; when she fled with her child into Egypt; when she found him in the Temple discoursing with the doctors; when during all his youth and young manhood he was beautifully obedient to his parents; when, after he had begun his career as a wandering teacher, at his word the water blushed into wine; when the reports came to her that he who had rested on her bosom and been haloed by

her arms was making the blind to
see, the lame to walk, and the dead
to live! Yet over all this period a
veil has been drawn. About all we
really see of Mary is at the Annunciation, at the Advent, at the Temple
when Jesus was twelve years old, at
the wedding where his first miracle
was performed, and — last of all —
when the tragedy was drawing to
its terrible end, when Jesus in the
midst of his unutterable agony com-
mends his mother to the care of his
dearest pupil and friend.

We know not what filled the years
between. Other children were born
to Mary, and one at least believed in
Jesus and became a bishop of the
Church at Jerusalem. How long she
lived we know not. She was a good

mother, and doubtless a true and no-
ble woman, who had been chosen like
many another for a work the greatness of which she felt but did not
understand.

The moment that Raphael has se-
lected for his great picture is when
she stands in sweet anticipation and
bewilderment, with her Babe in her
arms, dimly conscious that she is the
chosen of God, and glowing with the
joy of motherhood. And there was
another moment—the one which
comes some time to all, when earthly
hopes wither, when death sweeps his
raven wing over fondest anticipations,
and the earth and heavens are deso-
late. That moment has been chosen
by the great Hungarian Munkacsy in
his picture of "Christ on Calvary";

and it would be hard to imagine a scene of more pathetic beauty than that which he has painted, with the broken-hearted mother at the foot of the cross, clasping the feet of her Son, and on her hands resting her face, white with grief too deep for tears.

What shall be our attitude toward the mother of our Lord? Mary was a pure and beautiful woman, chosen of God for the holiest of ministries. And yet the apostle to whom Jesus committed her does not mention her in his memorial of the Master. "The divine wisdom . . . somehow took her aside with a set purpose not to let her mix her human-story products, beautiful and graceful as they were, with Christ's immortal life-word

from above. About all we can say
of her, therefore, under her embargo
of silence, is that she appears until
she disappears; which she does—
most wonderful, most nearly divine
of all human characters—in the still-
ness of a snow-flake falling into the
sea."[1] To all the ages she must oc-
cupy the highest place among women; fairer and purer than all the
lilies by which her maternity has been
symbolized, the one only woman to
whom a messenger from God spoke
such words as these: "Hail, thou
that art highly favoured. . . . Blessed
art thou among women!" If we do
not worship her with the Romanists,
we surely know that the greatest
honor that could come to a woman

[1] Bushnell's "Sermons on Living Subjects," p. 34.

was to be the mother of our Lord; we can exalt to the highest place those traits of purity, modesty, and fidelity, which alone qualified her for her ministry; and we can wait with the confident expectation that among the throngs which we shall some time see in spheres of light there will be none so near to our Master and Lord as she who was nearest to him upon the earth.

A study of the Sistine Madonna suggests the question, How could that woman be the mother of Jesus? She was a timid, beautiful soul who dwelt in obscurity, and who is known to the world only by the fact that she was his mother. She appears as a typical Jewish maiden at the first, and disappears at last with nothing to distinguish her from her countrywomen, a faithful Jewish mother, standing with breaking heart at the crucifixion of her Son. And the Son! Let us turn to him. Children always bear the characteristics of their ancestry; the law of heredity is as inflexible in the transmission of mental and moral as of physical traits. But what ancestry could even have suggested the birth of such a child as Jesus!

The Jews are a peculiar people all around the world. They have coherence, and power, and race loyalty, and mental and physical characteristics which time has not been able even to dim. This is more or less true of other races, but preëminently of the Hebrews. It is to their credit. But who ever thinks of Jesus as a

Jew — as belonging to any nationality? There is something about him
that appeals to the universal human
heart. The Roman world bowed at
his feet within three centuries after
his birth. All nations call him blessed.
He was unlike his ancestry in his
spirit and his teachings. His people
were narrow and exclusive; their
teachers were literalists, holding the
spirit of truth in bondage to the let-
ter; they thought that God loved
them and hated the rest of the world;
they looked on foreigners as on dogs.
But this Child, growing to young
manhood and dying almost before
he had passed the period of youth,
was broad and generous, utterly unlike the people from whom he came
and among whom he lived. His

sympathies embraced the world; he denounced the jealous teachings of the rabbis, and declared, with a boldness that seems almost preternatural, that neither at Jerusalem nor on Mount Gerizim alone was God to be worshipped, but that the universe was his temple. Without any training other than that mother could give— that mother with several children to care for and her household work to do—he enounced truths which differed from the teaching of his time as light from darkness; truths which from that day to this have been scattering clouds and bringing hope.

His people hated the publicans; he made a publican one of his first disciples. His people were accustomed to stone women who had sinned; he sat by a woman of this class, and before he told it to any one else told her that he was indeed the Messiah announced by the prophets and looked for by the Jews. His people made a fetish of the Sabbath day, teaching that it was a sin even to do good on that day; he said that man was more than any day. His people taught love to friends and hatred to enemies; he declared that hatred even to an enemy was of the nature of murder. His people exalted forms and ceremonies — the mere dress of things — to the dignity of religion; he brushed all these away, and declared that God looked to the heart and judged men by their motives. His people offered sacrifices until their Temple, splendid with marble and gold in the flashing of the sun, ran with blood and echoed with the shrieks of innocent animals; even under the shadow of that Temple he taught that sacrifices and ordinances were nothing, but a pure heart and a loving spirit everything.

On the canvas of Raphael are a mother and a child such as no other artist ever painted; the woman is the child's mother, and yet the Child seems not her child. The peculiarities of her race have left no impress on him. He is unlike everything by which he is surrounded. You might put Mary and Jesus down — away from Palestine — in Rome, in Paris, in Britain, among African savages, among South Sea Islanders; and everywhere the Mother would be

among strangers, and everywhere the
Child would be perfectly at home.
This is not true of any other of the
world's great teachers. Buddha, al-
though he taught eternal truths, was
a Hindu; his views of life were the
same as those of the elder religion in
India; he was a genuine reformer:
yet he appeals not to the world, but
to his own and kindred peoples. Ma-
homet was an Arab, and all his sys-
tem shows his nationality. Zoroaster
was a Persian, and his teachings are
so distinctly national that they have
almost died from among men. Moses
was the great Hebrew, and he, while
now and then suggesting the larger
spiritual kingdom which was to come,
was, after all, a Hebrew of Hebrews.

But what heredity accounts for Jesus? Was he the son of Joseph and Mary? Then the world's loftiest, purest, and most inspiring spirit, the one who has moved it most toward the life that all ages and nations acknowledge to be the true life, the divinest being that ever trod the earth, is the child of an obscure and ignorant carpenter who never emerged from his seclusion and a peasant woman whose years were passed in poverty and toil. It is like expecting from the huts around a mountain lake a being who, having spent almost all his life as did his parents before him, — working with his hands, — shall in the short space of eighteen months give to the world such visions of truth, and such glimpses of human possibilities, as shall change all the thoughts and aspirations of men. Is it not more in harmony with reason, more in harmony with what is known of nature and of life, to believe that Jesus Christ was the Son of God as no other human being ever was, than to think that that broad, generous, liberal, loving, inspiring, new-creating spirit had no parentage but that of two ignorant peasants, in an ignorant age, among ignorant people? This is the problem.

There stands the Mother, and there, in her arms, is the Child whose mysterious eyes read the far-away depths of the future. Was that Child the offspring of Jewish parents alone; or was he the Son of God? I have pondered that question long and earnestly. I have felt the force of the arguments against the divine origin of Jesus; but each day that I live and study the lessons he taught and the life he lived, each day that I see how those lessons and that life are leading all the nations more and more swiftly toward the goal of history,—the time when love shall rule on earth as it now rules in heaven,—only deepens the conviction which long ago became the faith of my life—that the only explanation of the character of Jesus, and of the change he is working in the world, is that the Son of Man is the Son of God, the Child of Mary is the Lord of Glory.

In Raphael's picture the angel faces are hardly less impressive than those of the Mother and Child. They throng the canvas; they make the clouds. What is their significance? Are they intended to suggest the angel chorus of the Advent night? They certainly make real to us the nearness of the spirit-life; and their sweet young faces, pressing close about the Baby Christ, suggest the blessed sympathy and ministry of the dwellers in eternal light. Indeed, but for the childlike simplicity of their cherub faces, I could rather think of them as seeking to explore the wonder and glory of the Advent. We are told in the Epistle to the Hebrews that angels desired to look into that mystery, but could not. The mystery about the person of our Lord has never been solved. He has expressly declared that it never can be explained. "No man knoweth the Son but the Father; neither knoweth any man the Father, save the Son and he to whom the Son will reveal him"; but how God reaches through humanity to save humanity is what no man knows: that is not a subject of revelation.

And this is not a mystery by itself. At the meeting of the Academy of Sciences of Berlin in 1881, when it was commemorating the birth of the philosopher Leibnitz, Du Bois Reymond delivered an address on "The Seven Riddles of Science." In that address he mentioned—and he spoke as a scientist—seven facts which had never received explanation, and which were then and are now apparently inexplicable, namely: the nature or essence of matter; the origin of motion;

the origin of life; apparent design in nature; the origin of consciousness; the origin of national thought and of language; the freedom of the will.

All the profoundest truths are mysteries: so says Religion; so says Science. But mystery is not synonymous with unreasonableness. We believe in the existence of life; we cannot explain it. We believe in the freedom of the will: we cannot explain it. We believe God to have been in Christ to save men: we cannot explain the Incarnation. Great truths that men live by all reach into the unseen. The test of a truth is what it does. Though a man deny the origin of motion, the fact of motion makes belief in it reasonable. Though a man deny the doctrine of the Word made flesh, the fact that it results in purer human living and a swiftly modifying and improving society makes belief in it reasonable. The problem of the Incarnation has never been solved, and never will be; and in that respect it is in line with the most vital and dominant facts of the universe. They transcend our human powers. They are accepted, not because they are mysteries, but because it is unreasonable to refuse to believe in them even though they cannot be explained. That Child in that mother's arms — who can tell how his work is done? Who can tell how that Babe whom the angels announced is binding all the nations with chains of love to the throne of God? But we believe in him and trust him precisely

because of what he is doing. We believe in the spring because the south
wind comes and breathes upon the
trees, and calls to the wild flowers,
and because the ardent sun kisses the
earth until its cold face ripples into
smiles; but how the spring comes,
who can tell? Who heard the voice
that summoned the south wind?
Who turned the hearts of the birds
northward? All this is unknown.
And we believe that that Child came
down out of heaven from God, not
because we can explain his genesis,
but because we have felt the thrills of
his life; because we have heard vocal
with his praise voices which once
sounded in orgies of shame; because
a redeemed humanity is rising in
white robes in response to the love

of God as revealed in the face and the life of that Child.

Let us get firm hold of this fact that even the blind can see: all truths in proportion to their greatness are mysterious; we accept them because we see what they do, not because we understand their nature or working. From the soft brightness of fleecy clouds in the wondrous picture, angels vainly seek to explore the mystery which no eye but God's can see into; and what angels see but cannot understand, you and I may accept and live by.

Raphael's Sistine Madonna has brought before us the Virgin Mother; the Child who was her child and yet not hers—whose heredity was from spiritual rather than from physical ancestry; and, as the consciousness of this great mystery has settled around us, we have remembered this other fact of superlative importance: that all the profoundest realities of life and thought, equally with the Incarnation, lift themselves to an altitude where they cannot be followed, while yet they prove their reasonableness by what they inspire in the experiences and before the eyes of men.

Mystery is the appropriate garment of divinity. Like Saint Sixtus and Santa Barbara in Raphael's picture, we adore and are silent before the ineffable glory.

OUR friend, our brother, and our Lord,
  What may thy service be?
Nor name nor form nor ritual word,
  But simply following thee.

We bring no ghastly holocaust,
  We pile no graven stone;
He serves thee best who loveth most
  His brothers and thy own.

In vain shall waves of incense drift
  The vaulted naves around;
In vain the minster turret lift
  Its brazen weights of sound:

The heart must ring thy Christmas bell,
  Thy inward altars raise;
Its faith and hope thy canticles,
  And its obedience, praise!

JOHN GREENLEAF WHITTIER.